What Should I Make?

What Should I Make?

by Nandini Nayar
Illustrations by Proiti Roy

TRICYCLE PRESS
Berkeley | Toronto

Neeraj's mother was kneading dough.
She was going to make chapatis.
She gave Neeraj some dough to play with.

Neeraj squeezed the dough.
"What should I make?" he said.

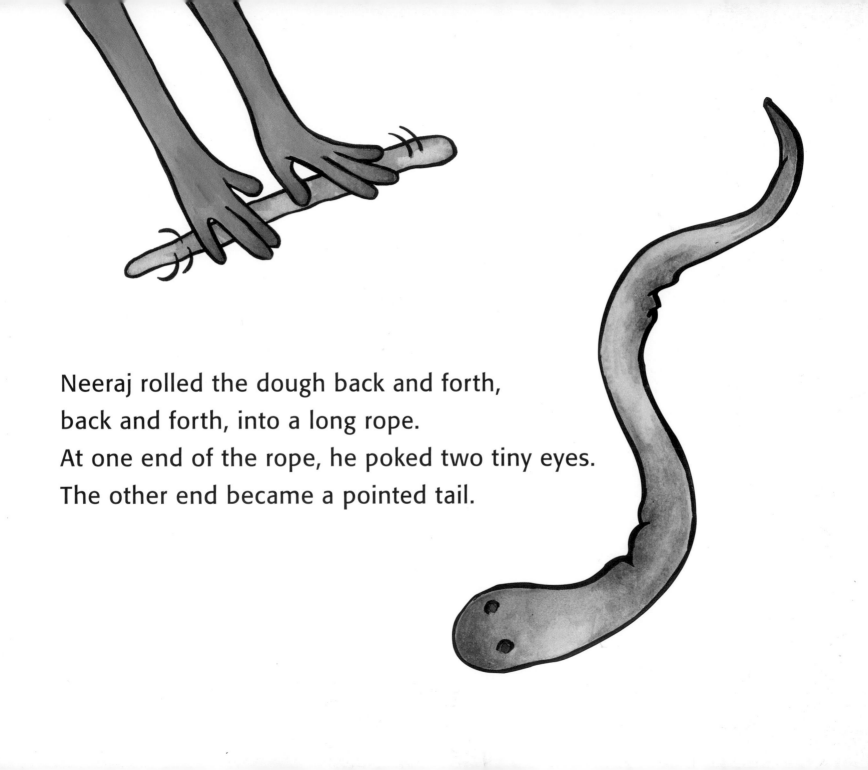

Neeraj rolled the dough back and forth,
back and forth, into a long rope.
At one end of the rope, he poked two tiny eyes.
The other end became a pointed tail.

"It's going to bite me!" Neeraj yelled.

"Roll it up, quick, quick!" his mother said.

Neeraj quickly rolled up the snake.

"What should I make now?" Neeraj said.

Neeraj rolled the dough into a ball.

He patted it down, poked in two tiny eyes, and pulled out a nose.

At the other end came a long tail.

"A mouse!
A mouse!"

Neeraj yelled, "It will run
all over the house!"

"Roll it up, quick, quick!" his mother said.

Neeraj quickly rolled up the mouse.

"What should I make now?" Neeraj said.

 Neeraj rolled the dough into a ball.

 He pinched off a small ball and stuck it on the big ball.

 He made round eyes and pointy ears.

He gave it a tiny nose and a tail.

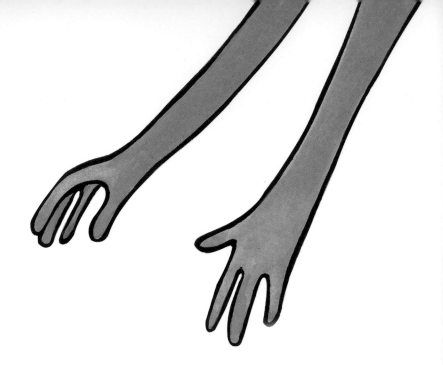

"A cat!
A cat!"

Neeraj yelled, "It's going to drink up all the milk!"

"Roll it up, quick, quick!" his mother said.

"I can't!" Neeraj said. "It's growing . . . and GROWING!"

"A lion!
A lion!"

Neeraj yelled, "It's opening its mouth!
And it's got big teeth!"

"Quick, quick!" his mother said. "You know what to do."
Neeraj grabbed the lion and rolled it up.
Round and round. Round and round.

He rolled the dough into a ball.
Round and smooth.

Then Neeraj pressed it flat.
A small circle.

Neeraj rolled the circle bigger and bigger. A big round chapati.

His mother put it on the *tava*.
It puffed up.

Squeezed.

Pinched.

Patted.

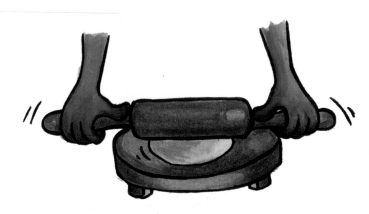

Rolled flat and round.

Hot, light, puffy.

It was the best chapati Neeraj had ever eaten!

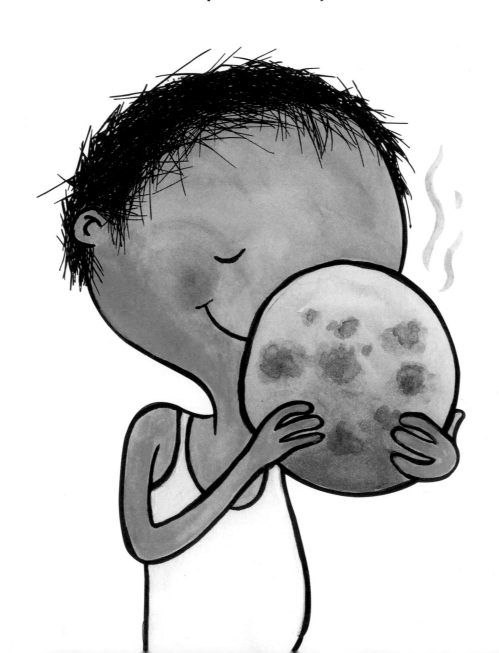

Making Chapatis

First, ask a grown-up to help you.

Pour half a cup of white flour and half a cup of whole wheat flour into a mixing bowl. Add a big pinch of salt to it and mix it all together. Keep a measuring cup of water ready.

Make a pit in the center of the flour. From the cup, pour a little bit of water into the pit.

Mix the water into the flour with your fingers. The flour will begin to stick to your fingers and hands. Don't worry, keep mixing.

Pour a little more water into the bowl. Keep adding water, little by little, and keep mixing.

As the flour comes together and begins to feel like dough, start kneading. (*Kneading* is gathering dough together into a ball and punching it down with your hands.)

Repeat this motion over and over for about a minute. Stop adding water when the dough is just a little sticky but stays together.

Knead the dough until it is a smooth, ball-like lump. Cover and set aside for a while.

After half an hour, the dough is ready to be made into chapatis.

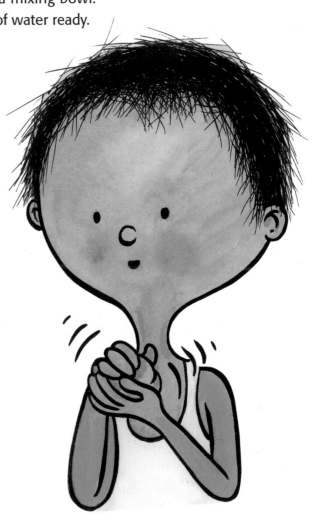

Pinch and tear off small bits of dough, and roll them with your hands into the size of ping-pong balls.

Spread out a large sheet of parchment or waxed paper to place the rolled-out chapatis on.

Now take a ping-pong ball shaped piece of dough, dip it lightly in dry flour, and roll it out with a rolling pin on a flat surface.

Roll all the balls into flat, round, thin pancake shapes. Place them on the paper.

Never mind if you make odd shapes. See if you can name the shapes!

When all the balls are flattened out and ready, ask a grown-up to heat a skillet or frying pan. When it is reasonably hot, place one flattened piece of dough in the pan.

Keep the heat at medium hot, not on high. An even heat is best.

Let the chapati cook for a bit on one side. You will see it change color, with bubbles popping up on the dough.

Then, with a spatula, turn it over. There may be a few dark brown or black patches on the chapati. That's natural.

Now watch it puff up like Neeraj's chapati! Remove it from the pan, and put the next one on.

Serve the hot chapatis with butter and jam. You can even eat them plain.

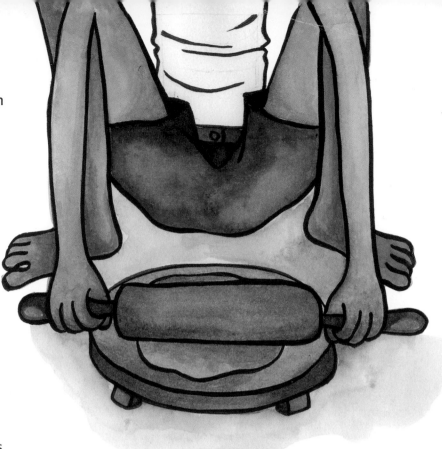

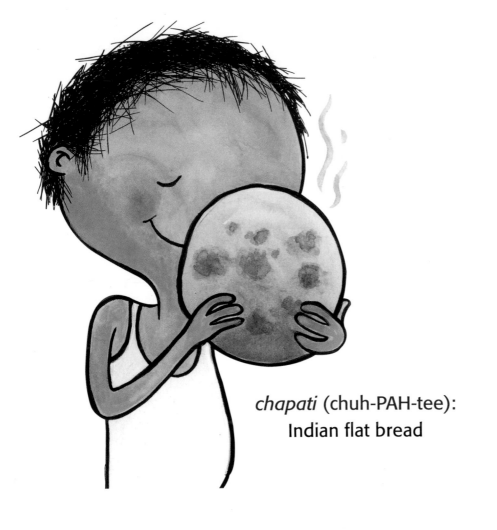

chapati (chuh-PAH-tee):
Indian flat bread

tava (tuh-VAH):
baking stone

This one is for Ai and her Neeraj — N. N.

Tricycle Press
an imprint of Ten Speed Press
PO Box 7123
Berkeley, California 94707
www.tricyclepress.com

Design by Chloe Rawlins

Typeset in Formata, Nobility Casual, and Providence Sans

Library of Congress Cataloging-in-Publication Data
Nayar, Nandini.
[What shall I make?]
What should I make? / by Nandini Nayar; illustrations by Proiti Roy.
p. cm.
Originally published: Chennai, India : Tulika Pub., 2007 under the title, What shall I make? simultaneously in English and Hindi.
Summary: While his mother makes chapatis, Neeraj transforms a piece of dough into different animals.
ISBN-13: 978-1-58246-294-3 (hardcover) | ISBN-10: 1-58246-294-1 (hardcover)
[1. Dough—Fiction. 2. Imagination—Fiction. 3. Mothers and sons—Fiction. 4. Cookery—India—Fiction.] I. Roy, Proiti, ill. II. Title.
PZ7.N216Wh 2009
[E]—dc22
2008042803
First published in 2006 by Tulika Publishers, 13 Prithvi Avenue, Abhiramapuram, Chennai 600 018, India
First Tricycle Press printing, 2009
Printed in China
1 2 3 4 5 6 — 13 12 11 10 09